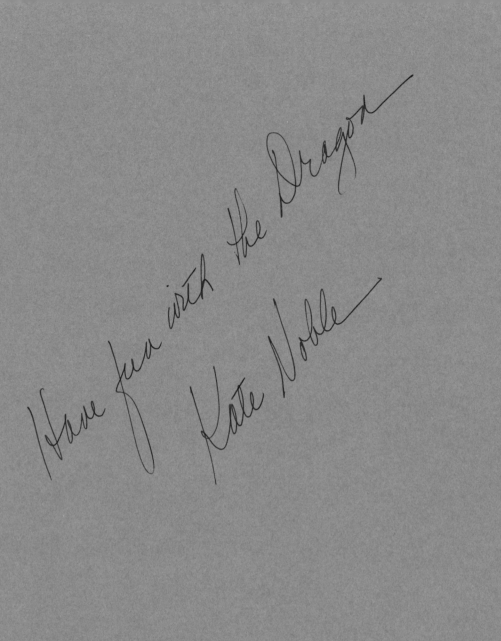

Have fun with the Dragon

Kate Noble

# The Dragon of Navy Pier

# The Dragon
# of
# Navy Pier

Kate Noble

Illustrations
Rachel Bass

Silver
Seahorse
Press

No part of this publication may be reproduced or transmitted in any
form or by any means, or stored in any information storage and
retrieval system without prior written permission of the publisher,
Silver Seahorse Press, 2568 North Clark Street,
Suite 320, Chicago, IL 60614

ISBN 0-9631798-5-3


First Edition
Manufactured in the United States of America
1  2  3  4  5  6  7  8  9  10

It wasn't easy being a dragon
on Navy Pier. Charlie sighed. The
carousel went round and round. It
was a beautiful carousel. He liked the
music. Beside him, he could see the
others going up and down, horses mostly.

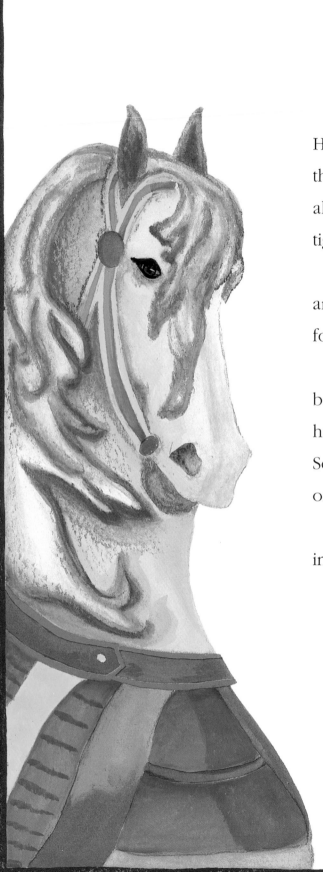

He didn't go up and down.
He stood still. All the animals in
the outside ring stood still. Up
ahead he could see a lion and a
tiger. They looked fierce.

Charlie wanted to go up
and down so he could be scary
for the children.

Dragons are supposed to
be scary. Little children sat on
his back, and that was fun.
Some of the older ones sitting
on horses pointed at him.

"Look," they said, with awe
in their voices, "it's a dragon."

He wanted to be able to leap into the air.

He wanted to be scary.

It was getting late now
and lots of the children had
gone home. The carousel
stopped for the night. Most
of the grownups were down
at the end of the pier
listening to music and
waiting for the fireworks.

Charlie was tired of
standing in one place.
He wanted to run. He
wanted to leap and dash
all the way out to the end
of the pier. He wanted
to look at the stars.

He had heard the sounds of
the fireworks. A POP and a soft
BOOM. Sometimes a KAPOW. If
he was facing the right way when
the carousel stopped, he could
even see some of the sparkles.

He longed
to watch the fireworks from the end of the pier.

He felt a funny tingling
in his leg. How strange! One
foot came loose from the rock
in front of him. What was
happening? Now the other foot.

Wow! He was loose. His
back feet too. What about his
tail? Could he move it? He
tried. It was loose too. He lifted
it and it fell with a thunk.

Charlie laughed. He threw
his head back. He was free. He
looked around at the others.
They were all sleeping. Well, he
wasn't sleeping. Not tonight.

He leaped off the carousel onto the sidewalk
and ran to the side of the pier. There was the
water and the boats and the stars. Charlie reared
up and looked at the sky. Would there be fireworks?

A woman screamed
and he whirled around.
She was pointing at him
and backing away. She
was afraid of him.

"Wow," Charlie thought,
"I'm a scary dragon." He
flapped his tail and loped
past the people.

They pulled back and left
him lots of space. He saw how
big and round their eyes
were. It was fun being scary.

He ran up to the
Ferris Wheel. People way up
high were looking down. He heard
a shout, "A Dragon. Look. It's a Dragon."
Charlie laughed. No, better not to
laugh. Dragons were fierce. He scowled
and ran on past the bands and the hot dog stands.

Sometimes he stopped and
reared up and looked ferocious.
Finally he was there, all the way
out at the end of the pier.
Then it happened.

Big bursts
like stars in the sky. Fireworks.
They were wonderful. Dragons love
fireworks. Charlie jumped up and
down. He waved his tail.

"Hello world," he shouted. "I'm
a dragon. I'm a fire-breathing dragon."

But was he? Charlie didn't know. He'd never even seen a fire-breathing dragon. He'd have to try.

He took a deep breath. He opened his mouth wide and blew the air out as hard as he could.

Fireworks! For the first time he was making fireworks of his own. He really was a fire-breathing dragon.

The people backed away. "It's a dragon," they almost whispered. "Look, it's a fire-breathing dragon."

When the fireworks were over
Charlie stretched and sat down.
The people started to clap their hands.
They were all looking at him.
"Wow," he thought, "they're
clapping for me." He laughed. He took a
bow. He nodded his head. Then he started
on the long way back to the carousel.

Charlie was tired. This fire-breathing was hard work. Time to get some sleep. People still pulled away from him, but they clapped as he went by.

He laughed and waved at them. A little girl, sitting on her father's shoulders, called out to him, "Are you really a dragon?"

He stopped and looked at her. "Yes," he said. "I'm really a dragon. I'm a fire-breathing dragon. My name is Charlie."

She laughed. "Hello, Charlie. My name is Lauren. Can I pet you?"

"Pet me? You mean like a dog?"

She laughed again. "Not like a dog. Like a dragon."

"Oh," Charlie said, "okay." He leaned his head toward her and she reached out and patted it very gently. Charlie liked it. It was nice to be petted. "That was nice," he said. Then he laughed and ran on down the pier.

He forgot
all about being
scary. This was
fun. Tomorrow
the carousel
would be fun too.
Tomorrow
night he'd come
out here again
and see the people
and work on his
fire-breathing.

Every night
after that Charlie
ran all the way to
the end of Navy Pier.
Even on nights when
no fireworks were
scheduled, Charlie
went out and
breathed fire.

People came
especially to see
him. They clapped
and they waved
and they laughed.

The dragon
of Navy Pier was
the happiest dragon
in all the world.